The Rescue Princesses
The Magic Rings

The palace was so silent that Lottie hardly dared to breathe. She felt her way to the bottom of the stairs, not wanting to switch the torch on in case someone saw the light. Her heart thumped in the darkness. *This is for the horses*, she reminded herself . . .

Have you read?

The Secret Promise

♥

The Wishing Pearl

♥

The Moonlit Mystery

♥

The Stolen Crystals

♥

The Snow Jewel

Look out for:

The Lost Gold

♥

The Shimmering Stone

♥

The Silver Locket

♥

The Ice Diamond

The Rescue Princesses
The Magic Rings

Paula Harrison

nosy crow

For Jennie, the best sister in the kingdom

First published in the UK in 2013 by Nosy Crow Ltd
The Crow's Nest, 10a Lant Street
London, SE1 1QR, UK

Nosy Crow and associated logos are trademarks and/or registered
trademarks of Nosy Crow Ltd

Text © Paula Harrison, 2013
Cover illustration © Sharon Tancredi, 2013
Interior illustrations © Artful Doodlers, 2013

3 5 7 9 10 8 6 4

A CIP catalogue record for this book is available from the British Library

Printed and bound in the UK by Clays Ltd, St Ives Plc

Papers used by Nosy Crow are made from wood grown in
sustainable forests.

ISBN: 978 0 85763 157 2

www.nosycrow.com

Chapter One

Royal Sisters

Princess Lottie spun round the bedroom as fast as she could, her red dress swirling. She twisted round and round, until she grew so dizzy that she collapsed, laughing, on top of the velvet blanket.

"Stop it, Lottie!" exclaimed Princess Emily. "You're squashing all the things I was just about to pack."

Lottie yanked a pile of creased clothes out from beneath her. Then she bounced up to peer into the enormous suitcase

1

that lay next to her on the bed. It was full of dresses, tiaras and a hairbrush with a diamond-studded handle.

"You can't fit anything else in there anyway," she said bluntly. "How much stuff do you need at your Royal School Thingy?"

"The Royal Academy for Princesses," Emily corrected her. "You have to have clothes for lessons, clothes for parties, clothes for ceremonies, and much more. I'll need all of these. There'll be ever so many special occasions to go to."

Lottie yawned. "Poor you! It sounds boring. I hope *I* don't have to go when I'm older."

Emily frowned. "It's important for every princess to learn how to fulfil her duties properly, you know."

Lottie chuckled. "You sound just like Mum." She put on a posh voice.

"A princess must perform splendid and magnificent duties, like spinning round as many times as she can before she falls over!" She leapt off the bed and started twirling madly again.

"Lottie! Stop it!" groaned Emily. Then she sat down on her bed and sighed.

Lottie stopped spinning and landed beside her sister, making the bed wobble.

"I suppose I do sound a bit like Mum," said Emily. "I still like having fun, though, and I'm going to be meeting up with my friends at the academy."

"I'll miss you!" Lottie gave her sister a quick hug. "Even though you like to moan!"

"I'll miss you as well." Emily grinned. "Even though you squash my clothes!"

Lottie looked at the mirror on the wall, where their reflections sat side by side.

Everybody always said it was easy

to spot that they were sisters, mainly because their hair was exactly the same red colour, like a flame. But while Emily's hair hung over her shoulders in loose waves, Lottie's was clustered into tight curls. Their eyes were different, too. Lottie's were a bright sparkling green while Emily's were a gentler hazel.

Lottie had always wished she was the older one. But now she was glad she wasn't leaving for school. Emily said the academy would be exciting, but Lottie wasn't so sure.

"If you've left any tiaras behind, can I borrow them while you're gone?" said Lottie, itching to look in Emily's wardrobe.

But Emily wasn't listening. She gazed thoughtfully at her sister, twisting a lock of red hair around her finger.

"Why are you staring at me like that?"

said Lottie. "I promise I'll put the tiaras back. I know I broke that silver one. But that was ages ago."

"There's something I need to tell you," said Emily slowly. "You know when you heard me and my friends talking about being Rescue Princesses when we were staying in Northernland?"

"Yes, it sounded like a really good game." Lottie pouted. "And I think you should have let me join in from the start."

"It wasn't a game at all," said Emily. "I was just worried that you were too little to know about it."

"I am NOT little!" Lottie burst out.

"I suppose not." Emily smiled. "Now that you've had your birthday, you're the same age as I was when I first became a Rescue Princess! Jaminta, Clarabel and Lulu have all sent me their magic rings, so I can explain that part, too."

"What?" Lottie nearly bounced off the bed. "What magic rings?"

"Hold on! I need to tell you everything from the beginning," said Emily. "Just listen! And try not to interrupt!"

Lottie frowned, but then decided not to be cross. After all, she wanted to know what Emily was going to say. "Tell me, then. What's this Rescue Princesses thing all about?"

Emily lowered her voice to a whisper. "Do you remember two years ago, when I went to Mistberg Castle for the Grand Ball? And you didn't come because you had chickenpox?"

Lottie nodded.

"Well, that's when I met the other princesses and we had our first adventure, rescuing the Mistberg deer from metal traps that had been left in the forest. It was really exciting, doing it all

by ourselves! After that we promised each other that we would always rescue any animals in danger. And we have, lots of times!"

Emily fumbled in her pocket and pulled out four rings, each with a beautiful heart-shaped jewel in the centre. The red, blue, green and yellow gems glittered in the palm of her hand.

"Your ruby ring!" said Lottie, picking up the glowing red jewel. "You always wear this one. Aren't you taking it to the academy with you?"

"No, I'm not, and you have to listen to me," said Emily urgently. "They'll send someone along for my suitcase in a minute and then I'll have to go."

"OK, I'm listening." Lottie fixed her green eyes on Emily.

"So the four of us became the Rescue Princesses, and we've rescued lots of

different animals all over the world.
Now it's your turn. I can't rescue animals
when I'm at school. You'll have to do it.
Find some other princesses, ones that you
trust, and do it together." Emily gazed
at her sister earnestly. "You'll have to do
what we did. Train hard, learn to climb,
swing and balance. Practise ninja
moves . . ."

"Ninja moves?!" Lottie's eyes grew even
rounder.

"Yes! Ally taught them to us. You know
that she used to be an undercover agent
before she came to work here. She's the
only other person who knows about the
Rescue Princesses."

"You really learned ninja moves?"

"Yes! And we used jewels with special
powers. We had quite a few of them, but
these rings are the only ones I can give
you right now." Emily dropped the other

three rings into Lottie's hand. "This green jewel is an emerald, the blue one is a sapphire and the yellow one is a topaz. We used them to contact each other when we were far apart. You have to press the jewel and speak into it when it lights up."

Just then, footsteps sounded in the corridor and the door handle swung slowly downwards. Lottie quickly hid the four rings behind her back and the girls held their breath. Ally, their maid, came in, carrying a pile of folded towels. The girls breathed out in relief.

"Are you nearly ready, Princess Emily?" said Ally. "Your carriage is waiting downstairs."

Emily closed her suitcase and zipped it up. "I'm ready now!" She turned to Lottie. "You will be sensible about this, won't you? Sometimes you rush off and do things without thinking."

Lottie pulled a face. "I'll be sensible!"

Emily smiled. "Goodbye, then! Look after those rings!"

"Bye, Emily!" Lottie gave her sister one last hug, and then Emily was gone.

Lottie watched from the upstairs window as Emily's carriage rolled away. She held the four rings tightly, with a fluttering feeling in her stomach. Now it was her turn to be a Rescue Princess. She would search out animals in danger and save them with fearless acrobatics and cunning ninja moves.

Emily had told her to be sensible. But that was just fussing over nothing. She had always been able to look after herself. She'd probably make a better Rescue Princess than her sister anyway!

Chapter Two

The Royal Dance Festival

Lottie leaned forward to look out of the tiny, square aeroplane window. It was a whole week since Emily had left for school. A whole week since she'd told Lottie about the Rescue Princesses! In that week Lottie had only managed to rescue one creature from danger and that had been a bumblebee buzzing round her bedroom. She'd just opened the window and let it fly away. It hadn't been very exciting.

But this place would be different. Down below, she could see rolling hills dotted with small patches of woodland. Surely there'd be lots of animals to rescue there, maybe rabbits or badgers or even a brown bear?

She was going to the Kingdom of Peronia with her mum, dad and Ally, to attend the Royal Dance Festival. Lots of royal families would be there. They would spend several days dancing and hold a grand performance on the final day.

Her dad smiled at her across the aisle of the plane. "We'll be there very soon, Lottie. Did you remember to pack all your dancing shoes?"

Lottie nodded. "Ballet shoes, tap shoes and jazz shoes for disco dancing."

"Ah, if only I was young again! Your mum and I really knew how to rock and roll," said the King of Middingland dreamily. "Our favourite dance was called the jitterbug!"

Lottie grinned at the thought of her mum and dad bopping about in their crowns and robes. She loved dancing and couldn't wait for the festival. But she wasn't just going there to dance. She was searching for princesses to join her, and they had to be girls that loved animals and adventure. She unzipped her shoulder bag and peeked at the four jewelled rings lying safe inside. She loved the ruby ring best, which was the one that Emily used to wear.

Checking that no one was looking, she picked up the ring and pressed the ruby firmly. Nothing happened. She sighed and put it back in the bag again. She had tried the ring several times now, but it would never light up the way that Emily had told her. Maybe Ally would know why it wasn't working.

The aeroplane landed on the runway. They all climbed down the steps and got into a polished silver car which would take them the short distance to the Peronian Palace. Lottie stared out of the window as the hedgerows flashed past, searching for signs of birds or animals that might need help.

After a while, a row of tall grey turrets rose above the hedge. They swung round a corner and the whole of the palace came into view. It was a magnificent place with an enormous arched front door. Lottie counted twenty-two turrets along the roof. It was certainly one of the grandest palaces she'd ever seen.

"Mum?" Lottie said suddenly. "There will be other princesses at this dance festival, won't there?"

"Of course," said her mum briskly.

"There will be plenty of princesses, and princes too. Just remember that *you* are from the royal family of Middingland, and must always behave with the utmost politeness."

Lottie nodded, her face lighting up. Plenty of princesses. That would mean plenty of *Rescue* Princesses!

They rolled slowly up the gravel driveway, passing a boy with muddy boots leading a beautiful sandy-coloured horse. The boy frowned at them, but Lottie was too busy looking at the horse to take much notice. She loved horses and spent hours grooming them in the palace stables back home in Middingland. This horse had been brushed till its coat shone and had lovely chocolate-brown eyes.

The car drew up at the front door just as a lady with a huge wide-brimmed hat came bustling out to meet them.

Lottie couldn't help staring at her hat. It was lime green and covered with purple plastic grapes.

"Here's Queen Sofia of Peronia! Please remember to curtsy, Lottie," said her mum.

"How wonderful to see you," boomed Queen Sofia.

Lottie climbed out of the car and performed her best curtsy. She knew it was a little wobbly, but at least she didn't fall over.

"Thank you so much for having us to visit," said the Queen of Middingland.

"Not at all! Now let me show you where you're staying." Queen Sofia led them into the palace, her lime-green hat bobbing as she walked.

The palace was full of royal visitors. Orange lamps glowed on the walls, lighting up huge paintings of soldiers

galloping about on horses. Queen Sofia
led them up a grand staircase and down
many corridors, until suddenly she
stopped.

"These are your rooms, my dears." The
queen patted Lottie on the head. "I hope
we'll see some splendid dancing from
you, my poppet. You look like just the sort
of princess to treat us to a bouncy jig!"

Lottie grimaced, but remembered just in
time that she was supposed to be polite.
"Umm, thank you," she said.

"Wonderful! Now, the Opening
Ceremony starts in half an hour," said
the queen. "I'll go and let you get settled
in."

While her mum and dad thanked
Queen Sofia, Lottie pushed open the door
to her room. It had a thick red carpet and
a large cuckoo clock hanging on the wall.
Lottie ran straight to the window and

pulled up the sash. The walls around the palace grounds were high, but she could still glimpse the countryside beyond. A cool breeze played with the curtains and birdsong drifted over from the nearby trees.

There was a knock on the door. Ally came in with her suitcase and set it down on the bed. "This is such a beautiful country," she said, seeing Lottie at the window.

Lottie smiled. "There must be lots of animals outside those walls and maybe some of them need help! I can't wait to go and explore."

Ally frowned a little. "I know Emily asked you to look out for animals in trouble, but your parents won't like it if you leave the dance festival too much." She opened the case and began unpacking dance skirts and ballet shoes.

"That's why I have to learn more ninja moves. That way I can sneak out without anyone seeing me." Lottie's eyes gleamed.

Ally smiled. "I think you'll be very good at ninja moves, once you've had a bit more practice."

"Oh! I just remembered. I have something important to ask you." Lottie unzipped her bag and poured the jewelled rings out into her hand. "These rings aren't working. Look, when I press them nothing happens." She pressed the ruby, sapphire, emerald and yellow topaz. But although they sparkled beautifully, none of them lit up or did anything exciting.

"That's odd," said Ally, looking closer. "I don't know much about Emily's special jewels. They have a magic all of their own."

Lottie tucked them away in the bag

again. "There must be a way to get them working. I'll just have to keep trying."

"You will be careful, won't you, Princess Lottie?" said Ally. "I don't want you rushing into something and getting hurt."

"Oh, don't worry!" Lottie said airily. "I won't get hurt. I never do!"

There was a knock at the door and her mum called her name.

"I'm nearly ready!" Lottie grabbed her best party dress from the suitcase and yanked it on. It was a deep crimson red and covered with lots of sparkly sequins. She picked up her favourite tiara, a zigzag one decorated with rubies, and rammed it on top of her curls. Then, shooting Ally a quick grin, she raced from the room, letting the door swing out wide behind her.

Chapter Three

Lottie's Dance Escape

The Opening Ceremony was held in a hall with a high ceiling. The walls were covered in spears and shields made from polished metal. Kings and queens clustered round, sipping tea and nibbling cake. Lottie followed her parents to the front of the hall and managed another curtsy to Queen Sofia, who was still wearing her lime-green hat.

While her parents chatted, Lottie scanned the room excitedly. This was her first chance to look for princesses to join her – princesses that wanted adventure.

She spotted one girl standing in a corner, wearing a long turquoise dress. The girl had brown eyes and straight black hair that fell right down to her waist. Lottie stared at her for a moment, but the other girl looked shy and turned away. She looked nice, Lottie thought, but maybe she was too nervous to be a Rescue Princess.

Then she noticed a second princess. This girl had dark hair that hung in loose curls, a yellow floaty dress and eyes that sparkled with excitement. She looked much more adventurous. But just then she bumped into a table, sending a pile of cherry cakes cascading to the floor. People ran forward, hurrying to pick them up. Lottie frowned; would a princess who was so clumsy really be good at animal rescues?

She scanned the room one more time. Her eyes stopped on a princess in dark blue with short blonde hair. But this girl was quarrelling with the boy standing next to her, pointing her finger straight at him and scowling. Lottie raised her eyebrows in surprise. She hadn't realised it would be so tricky finding princesses that seemed just right.

Just at that moment, Queen Sofia clapped her hands. "Your Royal Highnesses! Welcome to Peronia, and here's to a wonderful Dance Festival. Now we'll finish the Opening Ceremony with our first dance!"

Lottie's eyes sparkled. A dance! What would it be?

"Let's perform the Bobbing Dance," continued the queen. "Please form two straight lines."

Lottie stifled a groan. The Bobbing Dance was the one that her mum had made her practise before they left home. It was a long dance set to dull, slow music. All you did was bob up and down, and curtsy to the other dancers. It made her yawn every time she practised it. Why couldn't they choose something more exciting?

The kings, queens, princes and princesses arranged themselves into two long lines facing each other. Lottie stood at one end, near an open door which led out into the garden. Through the doorway, she could see green lawns and large flowerbeds full of tulips. She gazed out at them longingly.

A lady started to play a tune on the piano. The royal dancers began to bob up and down, and Lottie reluctantly did the same. But the hall was small for so many dancers. Two kings bumped into each other. Then the princess in the yellow dress stepped on Queen Sofia's toe, making her hop around holding on to her foot. The music stopped for a moment.

"Spread out please, Your Majesties! We don't want anyone to get hurt," called the lady at the piano. "Is everyone ready for the final part of the dance?"

Lottie ended up moving closer to the garden door as everyone tried to spread out. She could see more and more of the garden now. Beyond the tulips was a long row of fountains, and beyond that was a field with a sandy-coloured horse. The horse! Maybe it was the same one she'd seen when they arrived. She looked closer. The horse stood next to the fence, staring at the palace, as if it wanted to gallop across and dance with them.

Lottie giggled at the thought of the

horse joining in. She wished she could run over there and stroke it.

She twisted round to look at the dancing kings and queens. Maybe she could? No one had spotted that she was standing right by the door. If she sneaked out before the music stopped, then no one would notice her leaving. But she would have to be quick!

Her heart began to thump. She shot one last look at the dancing royals, and then dived through the open doorway. The bright sunlight was dazzling and her crimson dress billowed out around her legs as she ran. She passed the flowerbeds, where patches of red and gold tulips swayed in the breeze. She passed the row of carved fountains, where arching jets of water scattered spray over her head. The music from the hall faded behind her.

She stopped at the fence and tried to catch her breath. But the horse wasn't there any more. It was trotting away across the field.

"Come back!" called Lottie, but the horse tossed its mane and carried on trotting.

Lottie ran along beside the fence until she got to a gate. The horse slowed down as it reached a long brick building with a low roof. Lottie counted seven more horses inside, their heads looking out over their stable doors. Opening the gate, she walked across the rough grass towards the building. She smiled as she walked inside. It was dark in here and it smelled of hay. It reminded her of the stables at home.

The sandy-coloured horse stopped and turned back to nuzzle her shoulder.

"You're very friendly! What's your

name?" said Lottie softly, stroking the animal's nose.

"She's called Honey," said a voice from the shadows. "And *you* shouldn't be here."

Lottie spun round to see a boy leaning on the end of a broom and frowning at her. She recognised him as the boy she'd seen earlier, leading the horse up the drive. He looked even grumpier than before. But Lottie didn't mind about that.

"It's OK! I'm sure the grown-ups won't notice that I'm gone." She grinned widely at him. "This is a great stables. How many horses are there?"

The boy's frown cleared. "We have twenty-five of them. Actually twenty-six now, because one was born two weeks ago."

"A foal!" cried Lottie. "Where is it?"

The boy jerked a thumb over his

shoulder. "She's called Twinkle."

Lottie hurried up to the stall and peered over. A mare and her foal were lying down together on the hay. The foal was chocolatey brown with a white star on her forehead. She looked at Lottie and her soft ears twitched.

"She's lovely!" breathed Lottie. "She's the most beautiful foal I've ever seen!"

Chapter Four

A Foal Called Twinkle

"I'm Lottie, by the way," said Lottie.

"You mean, *Princess* Lottie," said the boy, looking at her tiara and her crimson dress, which now had bits of straw sticking to it. "And I'm Peter."

"Why don't I give you a hand with grooming the horses? I'm sure you could use the help." Lottie grabbed a body brush and a mane comb from a shelf nearby.

Peter grunted, which Lottie took as

a yes. So she brushed and combed the horses until their coats gleamed. She had just fetched a bucket to rinse the brush in, when she heard hooves drumming on the ground outside.

She went to see which horse was galloping so fast. But Peter appeared and shooed her back into the stables.

"It's Lady Slyden!" he hissed. "Don't come out or we'll both be in trouble!"

Lottie wanted to argue, but he seemed really anxious, so she didn't. She hid inside an empty stall and peered out through a narrow gap in the wooden slatting.

"Quickly, boy! I haven't got all day!" said a high-pitched voice.

"Yes, My Lady," mumbled Peter.

There was a loud neighing.

"Lazy animal! It went far too slow," snapped Lady Slyden. "I'll take a different one for a ride tomorrow morning. It can be that large black horse over there."

Lottie caught a glimpse of Lady Slyden as she climbed off the horse. She had a haughty look in her eyes and her mouth sat in a straight line, as if she never smiled. She wore cream jodhpurs and a navy jacket, and wore her hair twisted into a bun. She stared suspiciously at the stables for a moment and then stalked away, cracking her whip against the ground. Climbing into a large car, she drove off towards a narrow lane.

Peter came back inside. "I don't like lending her horses. I know she whips them too hard when she gets cross." He shuddered. "But Queen Sofia lets her borrow them, so there's nothing I can do."

"That's horrible!" cried Lottie. "If *I* see her using the whip too hard, I shall go and tell the queen straightaway."

A smile crept on to Peter's face. "You're not afraid of what anyone else thinks, are you?"

"I'm not scared of telling Queen Sofia what I see," said Lottie firmly. "Especially if it means I'm looking out for the horses."

"Well, thanks for helping to groom them," said Peter.

Lottie grinned. "It was really good fun! And now I think the foal needs some fresh air."

So Peter let her open the door of the stall where the mother and foal lay resting. The mare nuzzled the baby until she stood up on her wobbly little legs. The white star on her forehead stood out clearly despite the dim light of the stables.

"Come on, Twinkle," said Lottie softly.

"I'm going across the fields to fetch some more hay," called Peter. "I'll be back in half an hour."

Lottie waved goodbye to Peter and watched the foal follow her mother out into the yard. Her little tail swished with excitement when she reached the grass. Then she gambolled away, leaping round the meadow with her mane flying.

Lottie laughed and went over to stroke her. The foal whinnied and tried to nibble her ear.

"So you're called Twinkle," said Lottie. "You're very good at galloping for a foal that's only two weeks old."

Twinkle shook her mane and whinnied as if she agreed with everything Lottie said.

As Lottie reached up to scratch between her ears, a movement caught her eye. A lime-green hat appeared, bobbing along near the tulips. Queen Sofia was walking through the garden, leading a whole group of kings, queens, princes and princesses.

Lottie froze. While she'd been grooming the horses they must have finished their dancing and come out for a walk. She couldn't be seen with hay on her dress and mud on her shoes. She'd get in loads of trouble.

The queen's voice drifted over. "These are the best tulips for miles around! Have a good look at them and then I'll take you to see my wonderful fountains."

Lottie began to run back to the stables to hide, when she noticed the gate. Her heart missed a beat. The gate was wide open and swinging gently in the breeze. Had she left it like that? She didn't remember closing it after walking into the field. She frowned, cross at herself for being so forgetful.

Had any horses wandered out through it? She scanned the gardens. Two large horses stood by a fountain, bending their heads to drink from it. One was a dappled grey and the other was Honey, the sandy-coloured horse. She had to get them back into the field quickly. Soon all the kings and queens would turn the corner and see what was happening. Queen Sofia would not be pleased to find horses trampling her flowerbeds.

Lottie dashed over to the fountain. Peter was still fetching hay, so she would have to sort this out on her own.

"There's one more flowerbed of tulips to show you," said Queen Sofia. "Do come this way."

Lottie looked up, her heart racing. But no one appeared. Phew! The queen must have taken them in a different direction.

Hopefully that gave her a bit more time to catch the horses.

She reached the dappled grey horse and patted his side, urging him down the path and back into the field. Quickly closing the gate, she headed towards Honey, who was trotting further into the garden.

"Come back, Honey!" hissed Lottie, starting to chase her.

But Honey kept on going.

Lottie heard footsteps and turned round to find the princess with the dark curly hair and yellow dress running towards her.

"I've come to help you," panted the princess in yellow. "I'm Isabella. Don't worry; no one else has noticed that horse. They're all still looking at the tulips."

"Oh good!" said Lottie. "It'll be much easier to catch her with your help. If you

run one way and I run the other, then we can make her go back towards the gate. Ready?"

Isabella nodded.

So they crept down the path, trying to catch Honey. But the horse seemed to understand their plan and trotted away even faster, past a duck pond and a row of trees covered in blossom.

"Well, that didn't work!" said Lottie, pausing to catch her breath.

"Maybe one of us should distract her, while the other sneaks up?" said Isabella.

Lottie nodded; it sounded just like a ninja move. "That's a great idea. You get her attention and I'll sneak round."

Isabella started talking to Honey and clicking her fingers. Honey pricked up her ears and took a step closer.

Meanwhile, Lottie slipped to the side of the horse, patting her on the rump to make her walk forward. Finally they managed to coax her back down the path. As they rounded the last corner, the princess with the long black hair and turquoise dress was standing by the gate. She smiled and opened the gate to let Honey walk through.

The princess with short blonde hair stood there too, watching with her hands on her hips. "For goodness' sake!" she said, rolling her eyes. "Don't you know you shouldn't let horses wander around Queen Sofia's garden?"

"Of course I know that Queen Sofia
doesn't want horses in her garden!" said
Lottie crossly. "It was just an accident."

The princess with the blonde hair gave
a shrug.

Lottie gave Honey one final pat and
closed the gate behind her.

"Thanks for helping us," Isabella told
the princess dressed in turquoise.

"That's OK!" she replied. "We slipped
away from the grown-ups when we saw

what you were doing."

Isabella smiled at her. "I'm Isabella, by the way. I'm from Belatina, a kingdom of tropical rainforests."

The princess in turquoise smiled back shyly. "I'm Amina from Kamala, by the Eastern Sea."

Lottie grinned. "And I'm Lottie from the Kingdom of Middingland."

The princess with blonde hair took her hands off her hips and sighed. "I'm Princess Rosalind, from Dalvia in the cold North. We'd better get out of this mud and join the others before Queen Sofia notices we're missing."

"Just a minute," said Lottie. "I've got something to tell you. Actually, I've got an awesome princess secret to share and it will lead to big adventures." She paused dramatically.

"Ooh, what is it?" asked Isabella.

The sound of voices grew louder. Queen Sofia was just around the corner.

"I can't tell you yet." Lottie fixed them with her green eyes and lowered her voice mysteriously. "People might hear us. But if you come and meet me at nine o'clock tomorrow morning under those trees, I'll explain it all." She pointed at the trees covered with blossom.

"It had better not be boring," said Rosalind.

"It's *not* boring!" snapped Lottie.

"I'll come," said Isabella, pushing her dark curls over her shoulders.

"I will too," said Amina.

"Oh, all right, then." Rosalind rolled her eyes. "I'll come too."

"Great! It's going to be fan-tast-ic! You'll see," said Lottie.

Queen Sofia marched into view, followed by a crowd of kings and queens.

Lottie quickly edged behind Amina so
that they wouldn't see the mud splatters
and hay on her dress.

"Are you looking at the horses, girls?"
said the queen in a kindly manner.
"There are lots of lovely horses in my
stables. Some are very valuable because
they're racehorses and they've won lots
of prizes. That little foal might become a
racehorse one day, just like her mother
was."

The princesses nodded and curtsied and
then the group moved on.

Lottie beamed at Isabella, Amina and
Rosalind. These girls could make perfect
Rescue Princesses. Isabella seemed really
friendly and Amina, with her long black
hair, seemed lovely too. She wasn't quite
so sure about Rosalind.

The girls hurried over to join the back
of the group, which was now heading

towards the fountains.

"Oops! Sorry!" cried Isabella, as she tripped over a stone and knocked over three princes.

Lottie frowned. She hoped that the girls would be able to climb and run and balance. Her sister Emily's animal rescues had involved quite a lot of that sort of thing. Lottie was sure she could do it all (probably better than her sister). But what about the others? She crossed her fingers hopefully. Tomorrow she would find out what they could do.

♥

Lottie woke early the following morning, feeling full of energy. She took out the four magic rings, slipped the ruby one on to her finger and put the others in her dress pocket. Somehow it just seemed right that the ruby ring should be hers. She really hoped that something special would happen today and the jewels would start working. What was the point of having magical rings if they didn't do anything?

Tiptoeing carefully, she went downstairs to the dining room and out through the glass doors into the garden. Little white clouds chased each other across the blue sky, and even the grey turrets on top of the palace looked bright and cheerful.

When she reached the blossom-covered trees, Lottie found that Amina and Rosalind were already waiting. Rosalind was wearing a short blue dress and her blonde hair gleamed in the morning sunshine. Amina shifted from one foot to the other, her black hair swaying.

"Go on, then!" said Rosalind, not even bothering to say hello. "Tell us this amazing *Big Secret*."

Lottie looked at her sharply. "Where's

Isabella? I want to wait till everyone's here."

With hurrying footsteps, Isabella broke through the trees. "Sorry! Here I am!" she panted.

"Right, I think we should go a bit further away," said Lottie. "Follow me." She led them past the duck pond and round the edge of the horses' paddock.

Twinkle the foal came galloping across the field and stuck her head over the fence right next to them.

"Hello, Twinkle," said Lottie, stroking her velvety nose.

Twinkle shook her head and whinnied a greeting.

"What a lovely foal," said Amina. "She reminds me of my horse back home."

"She's very pretty with that white star on her forehead." Rosalind reached up to scratch between her ears.

Twinkle nibbled at Lottie's curly hair, making her giggle.

"She really likes you!" laughed Isabella.

Lottie saw Peter up at the stable yard and waved to him. "Let's carry on," she said. "We can always come and see Twinkle again on the way back."

So they walked on, crossing a stile into the next field and joining the narrow lane where Lady Slyden had driven her car the day before.

"Are we stopping soon? My feet hurt," said Rosalind.

"Let's go a bit further," said Lottie, leading them down the lane.

The fields on either side were full of sheep. Lambs frolicked across the grass, shaking their little woolly tails. The lane twisted and turned. Rounding a corner, the princesses found themselves by a stream with steep banks. Water tinkled along the stony river bed.

Lottie stopped and turned to face the others. "OK, we're far enough away from the palace now. But I need to ask you all something really important before we start." She paused, looking round at them. "Do you all love animals?"

Isabella, Amina and Rosalind nodded eagerly.

"My sister Emily started a secret club with her friends to rescue animals in trouble," said Lottie. "And when she went away to the Royal Academy for Princesses she handed it over to me. It's Top Secret and for princesses only. No princes or grown-ups allowed!"

Chapter Six

The Rescue Princesses Try-Outs

"I love secret clubs!" said Isabella, her eyes sparkling. "It would be great to rescue animals without any grown-up help."

Lottie grinned. "We'll be called the Rescue Princesses! If you want to join, you have to show me what you can do."

"What do you mean?" asked Amina. "Will it be tricky?"

"We'll be climbing trees and doing acrobatics and stuff like that. We'll do loads of training," said Lottie. "But for the try-outs we just need to find somewhere to test your skills."

"So what animals have you rescued so far, then?" said Rosalind.

"Only a bumblebee!" Lottie frowned at her. "But I've only just started." She glanced over at the stream. "Look! We can use that log over there for balancing on!"

The log bridged the gap between one bank of the stream and the other. The banks were high and there was a long drop from the log down to the water.

"All you have to do is walk across and back again." Lottie walked confidently along the log, placing one foot in front of the other. Halfway across, she suddenly realised how far she would fall if she lost her balance. But she held her breath and carried on.

"See! It's easy!" she told the others.
"Now it's your turn."

Isabella, Rosalind and Amina looked at
her doubtfully.

"What if we fall off?" said Isabella. "My
mum will be cross if I get wet."

"You'll be fine!" said Lottie impatiently.
"Come on!"

"I'll have a go." Amina put one foot on
the log. Then she skimmed lightly across
it and back again.

"Fantastic!" cried Lottie, making Amina
blush.

"All right, then!" said Isabella. "I'll
have a go too." But as soon as she began
to walk, the log wobbled alarmingly.
"Whoah!" she yelled, flapping her arms
to try and keep her balance.

Amina pulled her back on to the bank
again.

"Don't worry!" said Lottie, hiding her

disappointment. "It was only your first go! At least you had a try."

They all looked at Rosalind.

"I'm not sure I *want* to try out for your club yet," said Rosalind, folding her arms. "How do I know it will be fun?"

Lottie looked at her crossly.

"We'll make it fun," said Isabella. "*And* we get to help animals."

"And training together will be really cool. It's not all about balancing. I know someone who can teach us ninja moves!" said Lottie, crossing back over the log to join the other princesses.

The others stared at her, wide-eyed.

"Ninja moves!" Rosalind's blue eyes glinted. "I would definitely like to learn some of those!"

"And we each get a Rescue Princess ring." Lottie pulled the rings out of her dress pocket. "My sister Emily and her friends used them. If you press the jewel in the centre, it lights up and then you can send messages to each other." She held the rings out to show them.

"I want this one!" Rosalind grabbed the sapphire ring and pressed the jewel hard. "But it's not doing anything! Maybe your sister was making it up."

Lottie glared at her. "She wouldn't do that! I don't know why they're not switching on yet. But maybe we all have to be wearing them at the same time. Maybe that's how they work."

"I'd like this one, please." Isabella picked up the yellow topaz.

"Thank you, this is beautiful," said Amina, taking the emerald ring.

"And I've got the ruby one," said Lottie, showing them hers.

The princesses slid the rings on to their fingers and gazed at the sparkling jewels.

Rosalind pressed the sapphire with her finger. "It still isn't working."

Lottie pressed her ruby, but nothing happened.

"Mine's not working either." Isabella stared at her yellow topaz, and Amina also shook her head.

Lottie frowned. "I don't understand. I'm sure they should be lighting up by now." She shook her head. What could be going wrong?

"Maybe you broke them on the way here," said Rosalind.

Lottie flushed angrily. But before she could reply, a thundering noise swept down the lane. The princesses looked round, unsure which way it was coming from. It grew louder. The ground began to shake.

"What's that?" called Isabella.

Amina turned pale.

"Come this way!" yelled Lottie, trying to get them to hide.

But before they had time to move, a huge dark shape burst round the corner and rushed towards them.

Rosalind let out a shriek, which made the dark shape rear up, and two massive hooves flailed in the air above them.

Lottie caught a glimpse of a figure with tall riding boots and cream jodhpurs, sitting on top of the giant animal.

"Don't worry!" she called to the others. "It's only a horse. It'll be all right." But her words were drowned out by a loud neighing and the cracking of a whip.

Isabella, Rosalind and Amina started running up the lane towards the palace garden.

"Wait!" shouted Lottie, but the other princesses didn't even look back.

The black horse calmed down and

shook his bridle restlessly.

"Silly girl!" snapped the rider, in a haughty voice. "You shouldn't be sneaking about outside the palace. You nearly caused an accident."

Lottie jumped, recognising the voice of Lady Slyden, the woman she'd seen at the stables yesterday.

"Don't stand there staring at me!" ordered Lady Slyden. "Get back to the palace like your silly friends." She glared at Lottie, cracked her whip and sped away without waiting for a reply.

Lottie watched her go. Then she turned slowly and walked back towards the palace.

As she went past the paddock, Twinkle trotted along and put her head over the fence again. Lottie stroked the little foal's nose. But her heart felt heavy. Not because of Lady Slyden's rudeness, she didn't care about that. She was disappointed that the other princesses had rushed off so quickly. As soon as they had seen danger, they had all run away.

Chapter Seven

The Princesses' Dance Routine

When Lottie reached the palace, lunch was being served in the dining room, with its large glass doors that opened out into the garden. Waiters brought around platters of delicious pizza, followed by apple pie and ice cream.

Lottie ate hers silently.

"Are you all right, Lottie?" Her mum looked surprised to see her so quiet.

Lottie nodded. "Can I have some more chocolate ice cream?"

"I suppose so!" Her mum laughed, passing some to her. "Oh, you're wearing Emily's ruby ring. It was nice of her to give it to you."

Lottie nodded again. The ruby ring just reminded her of all that had gone wrong this morning. The jewels weren't working and the other girls didn't seem to understand what being a Rescue Princess was really about. But *she* was still determined to help animals in trouble, even if she had to do it on her own.

♥

After lunch, Queen Sofia divided all the kings, queens, princes and princesses into groups ready to learn new dances. She gathered Lottie, Isabella, Amina and Rosalind together.

"It would be wonderful if you four princesses would do a dance on the final day of the festival," she boomed. "Would you like to do that?"

The princesses nodded.

Queen Sofia glanced at a group of princes who were mooching about in a corner. "Perhaps you could make up something that involves those princes too. You could all hold hands as you dance. That would be nice!"

"No!" cried Lottie and Rosalind together.

"I mean, I don't think that's a very good idea, Your Majesty," Lottie added. She could see that Rosalind was just as horrified as she was at the queen's suggestion. The two girls exchanged a grin. Maybe Rosalind wasn't so bad after all, Lottie thought.

"I think the princes might want to dance by themselves," said Amina quietly.

"Very well, then!" Queen Sofia handed

them a CD player. "If you go along the corridor you'll find a room that is suitable for practising your dance. There's some music to choose from on the window sill."

The girls curtsied and hurried away. At the end of the corridor, they found a large sitting room full of sofas and armchairs. Lottie set the CD player down on the window sill and turned to face the other princesses. They were all still wearing their rings, she noticed.

"We're sorry we ran off before," Isabella told her. "Once we stopped running, we realised that it must have been a horse that suddenly came round the corner. But it was so huge and it galloped so fast!"

"That's all right," said Lottie, forgiving them instantly.

"We still want to join the Rescue Princesses," added Amina.

"Especially if you can get these rings to

actually work," said Rosalind.

Lottie pressed the ruby in her ring again. "They are supposed to work. You'll just have to believe me."

"I believe you," said Isabella.

Lottie smiled back at her. "I suppose we'd better get on with this dance for Queen Sofia. What kind of dance shall we do?"

"A tap dance!" cried Isabella.

"Disco!" said Rosalind firmly.

"I quite like ballet," said Amina.

"Let's play some of this music and work out what we like best." Lottie switched on the CD player and fiddled with the buttons.

The girls pushed the sofas and armchairs towards the walls to give themselves more room. Then they listened to several pieces of music, kicking off their shoes and trying out some dance moves.

"Actually, I really like this pop song!" Isabella jiggled around, nearly crashing into a bookcase.

"I do too!" Lottie clicked her fingers to the rhythm. "I often play this at home."

Amina nodded. "Let's do our dance to this one, then."

"We could start with our arms together and then move them like this." Lottie showed them her dance move.

"Then we go, step together, step and turn." Isabella's face lit up as she danced.

The door opened and Ally came in. "Hello, princesses! Queen Sofia sent me to see how you're getting on. Do you need help with anything?"

"We're fine thanks, Ally," said Lottie. "We've nearly finished sorting out the dance routine."

"But we haven't decided on what

costumes or dance shoes to wear," said Rosalind. "I think we should wear dresses that match."

"I don't think it matters that much if we wear different costumes," said Lottie.

"Well, I think it does!" Rosalind put her hands on her hips.

"It would be nice if our dresses were the same," said Amina, pushing back her long hair. "And we need our jazz shoes. We can't perform barefoot."

"Queen Sofia has a whole cupboard full of costumes upstairs," said Ally. "Why don't I go and see if there's anything in the right size? Then I'll collect your jazz shoes on the way back."

"Great idea!" said Isabella.

"Thanks, Ally," said Lottie.

Ally smiled and hurried away to look for the costumes.

"All right, then! Let's go back to the

beginning and see how the dance goes so far." Lottie went over to the CD player and pressed the buttons to take the music back to the start. "I'll just open the window. It's getting really hot in here." She pulled up the window sash to let in the breeze.

"And one, two, three and spin!" Isabella counted to herself as she practised the dance moves.

Lottie leaned over the machine, wondering why the music hadn't come back on. Had she pressed the wrong button? Just as she was about to try again, a high-pitched voice floated up through the open window.

"You shouldn't have come here! I told you – we meet at midnight!"

Lottie's ears pricked up. This seemed like a very strange thing to say. Why would someone be meeting at midnight?

She leaned forward, peering down to see who was talking below.

"What are you doing?" said Rosalind.

Lottie swung round and put a finger on her lips to signal the others to whisper.

Someone else spoke below them. It was a man's voice this time. "But, My Lady! I couldn't remember where I was supposed to park the van. So I had to come and see you."

"We've been through this over and over again! Park it by the stream on the corner of the lane, then walk up to the stables to help me," said the high-pitched voice.

With a sudden shiver, Lottie realised that she knew who it was. That voice belonged to Lady Slyden, the woman who'd been so rude to her that morning.

Leaning out a little further, she could see it was definitely Lady Slyden, still wearing her cream jodphurs and with her hair twisted into a bun.

"What are we looking at?" whispered Isabella, as she and Amina joined the other two girls at the window.

Lottie pointed silently at Lady Slyden and her servant standing in the garden below.

"How many horses are we taking?" said the man. "It's not a very big van, you know."

"Hush, fool! Are you trying to tell my plans to the whole palace?" snapped Lady Slyden. "You'll fit in as many horses as I tell you to. Now, go away! I don't want to see you again till midnight."

Lottie's head was buzzing. Why were they talking about putting horses into a van? And why were they doing it at midnight?

Chapter Eight

The Wicked Lady Slyden

The princesses held their breath as they watched Lady Slyden disappear along the garden path.

"What was all that about?" said Rosalind at last. "Why are they meeting at midnight?"

"That was Lady Slyden, the woman riding the black horse this morning," said Lottie grimly. "And if she's moving horses around in the middle of the night, I think it sounds very suspicious."

Isabella's dark eyes widened. "You don't think she's trying to steal Queen Sofia's horses, do you?"

"The queen did say that she has some very valuable racehorses," said Amina. "They're probably worth an awful lot of money."

"Poor horses!" said Lottie. "Peter, the boy from the stables, says that Lady Slyden is mean to them. She whips them too hard when she gets angry."

The other girls looked shocked.

Lottie gazed through the open window at the horses' paddock just beyond the garden. There were lots of horses out in the field, including Twinkle, who was frolicking round and round in circles. Even from far away, Lottie could see how much the foal was enjoying the fresh air. She skipped around, only stopping to shake her mane and flick her tail.

Lottie lifted her chin and marched over to the door. "I'm going to tell Queen Sofia about this right now!"

"You can't!" gasped Amina. "What if she thinks you've made it all up?"

"She has to be told what Lady Slyden's up to," said Lottie. "The horses are in danger."

"Good! I'll come too!" said Rosalind.

Lottie and Rosalind dashed down the corridor, with Isabella and Amina close behind them. They ran into the hall where the Opening Ceremony had taken place the day before. Queen Sofia was sitting on a large wooden throne talking to a group of young princes.

"No one expects you to do a dance that's too difficult," she was saying to them. "Try practising the hornpipe! All you have to do is fold your arms and hop on one leg."

Lottie felt a little less sure of herself now that she was right in front of the queen. She took a deep breath. "Your Majesty!" she called out. "We've got something really important to tell you!"

"It's about your horses," added Rosalind.

"Horses?" Queen Sofia looked at the princesses and shook her head, making her lime-green hat wobble. One of the young princes giggled, but she took no notice. Instead, she rose from her throne and towered over the girls.

"Princesses!" she said sternly. "Just look at yourselves! You should be walking and curtsying like proper young ladies. But instead you RAN in like PUPPIES. Your hair is a MESS and you have BARE FEET!"

There was silence. The princesses stared at their bare feet.

"But, Queen Sofia," began Lottie. "We

were just waiting for Ally to come back with our dance shoes and we heard . . ."

"Enough!" cried the queen. "I shall not listen to anyone who comes in with bare feet."

So the princesses slunk back out of the hall, not daring to speak until they reached the corridor.

"That was terrible!" cried Isabella. "What shall we do?"

"What's the matter, princesses?" Ally hurried up to them, carrying lots of dance shoes and an armful of dresses.

"We think that Lady Slyden is planning to steal some of Queen Sofia's horses. We tried to tell the queen, but she wouldn't listen to us," said Lottie, and she explained what they had overheard through the open window.

Ally's forehead creased with worry. "I don't trust Lady Slyden," she said at last.

"And I know she doesn't treat horses very well."

"Then we have to go to the stables at midnight and stop her," said Lottie.

The princesses looked at each other.

"But what if the kings and queens catch us sneaking out?" said Amina, her black eyes wide. "Maybe we should try talking to Queen Sofia again."

"There's no point," said Rosalind. "She wasn't listening."

"Leaving the palace at midnight will be scary," Isabella looked solemn. "But for the sake of the horses we have to try."

"I can help you get away from here without anyone seeing you," said Ally. "But for now you'd better go and get changed. It's nearly time for the banquet."

The princesses rushed back to their rooms to get changed. Lottie took a long red dress dotted with sequins out of her wardrobe. She put it on and added a golden crown decorated with rubies to match her ruby ring. Her green eyes sparkled back at her from the mirror.

Just then, the cuckoo clock on the wall chirped six o'clock. Lottie hurried out of her room and caught up with the others at the top of the stairs. Isabella turned round and smiled as she saw Lottie coming. Her yellow dress floated out at the hem and a swirly gold tiara gleamed on top of her dark curls.

Rosalind and Amina had put on their best clothes, too. Rosalind wore a dark-blue dress and her tiara was studded with the biggest emeralds that Lottie had ever seen. Amina's turquoise dress was tied in an elegant knot at one shoulder and her tiara was made from arching loops of silver.

"We've seen Lady Slyden," hissed Rosalind, pointing at the hallway below.

"She's talking to Queen Sofia," whispered Amina. "How can she act so friendly when she's planning to steal her horses?" She leaned in for a closer look, her long black hair hanging over the bannisters.

"She's just pretending to be nice," said Lottie darkly. "I think we should keep an eye on her."

So the princesses kept an eye on Lady Slyden throughout the first course of the banquet, which was soup with buttered rolls, and they watched her during the main course that followed. Lady Slyden rose from her seat and disappeared just as the sticky toffee pudding was served.

Lottie cast a worried look at the other princesses. Lady Slyden must be going to get ready for tonight.

"Mum? Can I go back to my room? I'm tired now," said Lottie.

The Queen of Middingland raised her eyebrows. "And miss the sticky toffee pudding? Are you sure you're feeling all right, Lottie? No, you must stay here and sit up straight. It's important for you to practise behaving nicely at banquets."

Lottie sighed and tapped her spoon on the table. How could sitting still at banquets be important when there were ninja moves to learn and horses to save?

Chapter Nine

Ninjas in the Palace

At last the banquet ended. The princesses raced up to Lottie's room, where Ally showed them how to move around without being seen. Then they practised tiptoeing stealthily up and down the corridor.

"I want to learn more ninja moves. This is so much fun!" cried Rosalind, flitting past like a shadow.

"I've heard that there's a book which contains every single ninja secret inside it," said Ally. "It's called *The Book of Ninja* and it's said to have been lost for a long time."

"I wish I could find it and read it," said Rosalind.

Isabella tripped over a wrinkle in the carpet and fell to her knees. "I don't think I'll ever be good at this!" she gasped.

"You're doing very well, Princess Isabella," said Ally. "Maybe a mug of hot chocolate would help."

Ally went downstairs and reappeared after a few minutes with a tray. The princesses sat on Lottie's bed to sip their mugs of hot chocolate. Lottie looked at the cuckoo clock on the wall. It was only half past eight. There were still hours to go till midnight.

"I've got a great idea!" exclaimed Amina, staring at the pile of dance costumes that Ally had left on Lottie's bed. She put down her mug and began sorting through the leotards and skirts. "These dance dresses that Ally found for us – if we wear a dark colour tonight, then no one will see us in the shadows." She pulled a shiny black dress out of the pile.

"Good idea! And we could put them on underneath our nightdresses when we go to bed," said Isabella.

"Here are some more of them." Lottie handed out the dresses so that they had one each. "You're right, Amina. This will make it much easier to reach the stables without anyone seeing us."

"But when we get there, how will we stop Lady Slyden from taking away the horses?" asked Rosalind.

Lottie thought for a moment. "I don't know," she said. "We might be able to distract her. We'll have to think quickly."

There was a knock at the door and the princesses hid the black costumes behind their backs. The door opened and Lottie's mum came in.

"It's time for bed, all of you," said the Queen of Middingland, smiling. "It will be a busy day tomorrow, full of excitement. So you need plenty of rest. Sleep well!"

"We will!" chorused the princesses.

When the queen closed the door again, they collapsed laughing on the bed.

"It will be a lovely night of rest, full of ninja action!" giggled Isabella.

At last, Lottie managed to stop laughing. "You'd better go before my mum comes back. Don't forget your black dresses. I'll meet you at the bottom of the stairs at ten minutes to midnight."

Lottie lay in bed, staring at the clock. The

minutes ticked by very slowly. Her eyelids began to close.

"Cuckoo!" The bird inside the wooden clock popped out and chirped eleven times.

Lottie sat straight up. She must have fallen asleep. Thank goodness for the cuckoo clock. She jumped out of bed and pulled off her nightdress to reveal the black dance dress underneath. There was less than an hour to wait now. Maybe she should get her torch ready.

She grabbed it from the bedside drawer and switched it on and off a few times under the covers. Then she took off her ruby ring and turned it over in her hand. If only the rings were working! She could have sent a message to the others. She tapped the ruby with her fingernail. But nothing happened. She rubbed it against her pillow. Still nothing.

She looked at the clock again. Half
an hour to go. She frowned. It wasn't
just the rings that were bothering her.
What if Isabella tripped over something
again? What if Amina got scared? And
what if Rosalind started arguing about
everything? There were so many things
that could go wrong.

Finally, at quarter to twelve, she slipped
on her shoes. Her bedroom door made a
loud creak when it opened. But somehow
she managed to close it again quietly and
creep down the passageway.

The palace was so silent that she hardly
dared to breathe. She felt her way to
the bottom of the stairs, not wanting
to switch the torch on in case someone
saw the light. Her heart thumped in
the darkness. *This is for the horses*, she
reminded herself. She couldn't let them
get stolen by the horrible Lady Slyden.

Three more princess shadows slipped down the stairs to join her. The black dresses worked well, thought Lottie. The others were hard to spot in the dark.

"Is that you, Lottie?" murmured Isabella.

Lottie switched on her torch. "Yes, it's me!" she whispered. "Are you ready?"

The others nodded.

Lottie flicked the torch off again. The princesses tiptoed into the dining room and unlocked the doors that led outside. The garden was lit by a silver crescent moon which bobbed on a sea of clouds. Now they just had to cross the garden without being seen.

Remembering their ninja training, the princesses looked around for good places to hide. Then they ran across the lawn one by one, darting behind trees and statues. Lottie's red curls bounced as her

feet flew over the damp grass. She joined the others by the gate to the horses' field and tried to catch her breath.

She looked at her new friends, doubt creeping into her mind. Were they really going to be able to help the horses? Isabella had already tripped over a plant pot and Amina looked terrified.

"There's no sign of Lady Slyden or her servant yet," said Isabella, scanning the fields.

"Maybe they're already inside the stables." Amina's voice wobbled a little.

"They can't be. We'd be able to hear them," said Rosalind.

The princesses listened hard. The trees rustled and an owl hooted a long way off.

"You're right, they can't be here yet," said Lottie. "Let's go round the back of the stables. That way we'll be completely hidden before they arrive."

They crept across the stable yard. Isabella tripped over an animal's drinking trough, which made a loud clatter.

"Shh!" said Rosalind.

One horse put his head over the stable door and snorted.

Lottie stopped suddenly. "Why aren't there more of them?" she asked.

"What do you mean?" said Amina nervously.

"There's only one horse looking out of the stables," Lottie pointed out. "There should be more."

"Maybe the others are all asleep," said Rosalind.

Lottie went to look over each stable door. A cold dread rose inside her as she counted the empty stalls. There were five horses in the front stalls. She was sure there had been more than that yesterday.

She ran into the stables, checking the inside stalls one by one.

"Come back!" hissed Rosalind. "They'll see us if we hide in there."

Lottie ignored her. With a racing heart, she peered over into Twinkle's stall and flicked on her torch. The foal's mother was standing up, tossing her mane anxiously. But the little foal was gone.

Somewhere in the distance, a clock chimed midnight.

The other princesses ran into the stables to join Lottie. Rosalind grabbed the torch and shone it all around.

"What is it, Lottie?" cried Isabella. "You look awful!"

Lottie blinked back her tears. "We're too late! Lady Slyden's already been here and she's taken Twinkle."

Chapter Ten

Finding Twinkle

"We *have* to go and tell Queen Sofia what's happened," gasped Amina.

"We can't! If we go back to the palace now that gives Lady Slyden more time to get away!" said Lottie. "Anyway, how can we wake up the queen in the middle of the night?"

There was a moment of silence. No one liked the idea of waking up Queen Sofia.

"We could try to follow Lady Slyden and the horses," said Isabella. "Do you think we'd catch up with them?"

Lottie's green eyes flashed. "I'm going to try. Who's coming with me?"

"I am," said Amina quickly. "I can't believe they took a little foal away from its mother. They should be ashamed of themselves."

"I'm coming too," Isabella said firmly.

Rosalind put her hands on her hips. "Well, I'm not letting you all have an adventure without me!"

Lottie grinned and held out her hand. "Then we're Rescue Princesses together!"

Isabella, Amina and Rosalind placed their hands on Lottie's, one on top of the other. The heart-shaped jewels in their rings lit up with a sudden glow, which lasted for a few seconds and then went out.

"Awesome!" cried Isabella, staring at the jewels.

"We finally made them work," Rosalind said softly.

"Now we're proper Rescue Princesses!" said Lottie, her eyes sparkling. "Come on, let's go! We've got to catch up with Lady Slyden!"

The circle of light from Lottie's torch led the way as they raced across the field. They slowed down as they reached the narrow lane.

"We don't know where they are," said Rosalind. "We could be going in the wrong direction."

"Lady Slyden told her servant to park his van by the stream," Lottie reminded her. "So I think they must be this way."

They sneaked down the lane until Lottie stopped them. She held a finger up to her lips.

They could hear voices.

They crept closer and hid next to the

wall on one side of the lane. A few metres away, a man struggled with a tall stallion that had reared up on its hind legs. He was pulling it towards a black van.

"The horse doesn't want to go into the van," whispered Amina.

"Get in there now or I'll get my whip out!" hissed Lady Slyden.

"How dare she?" whispered Lottie furiously. "I wish Queen Sofia could see this!"

The man finally managed to pull the horse into the van.

"That's the last one, My Lady," he said, climbing out of the van and closing the door.

"Good!" said Lady Slyden. "Get out the map and I'll show you where you're driving to. You must get there as fast as you can."

"But, My Lady! I can't drive too fast in

case it upsets the horses."

"You will do as I say!" snapped Lady Slyden.

The servant and Lady Slyden walked to the front of the van and bent over a large map.

The princesses exchanged looks. This was their chance! They tiptoed across the lane towards the stream. When they were sure that no one was looking, they dashed out of the shadows and hid behind the van.

Rosalind shaded her eyes to look through the little window in the van door. "The poor horses are really squashed in there."

"Let's get them out," whispered Amina.

Lottie pulled gently on the handle, opening the door without a sound. There were four fully grown horses inside and Twinkle, the little foal. The animals

looked at the princesses with big dark eyes. Twinkle began to shiver.

"Poor things! They're really scared," said Amina.

"What shall we do? If we get the horses out, Lady Slyden will hear the sound of their hooves on the road," said Isabella.

"I know! I'll use my new ninja moves," said Rosalind. "I'll sneak further down the lane and do something to get their attention."

"Please be careful!" said Amina.

Rosalind flitted away into the darkness. Lottie peered around the side of the van. Lady Slyden and the man were still leaning over the map.

Then out of the darkness came a very loud clanging, like someone hitting a tin can with a stick. Lady Slyden's head jerked up. She left the map at once and crept down the road towards the noise.

Her servant followed her.

"I hope Rosalind knows what she's doing," said Isabella, with a shiver.

"Now's our chance!" hissed Lottie. "Quickly! We've got to get these horses to safety."

Chapter Eleven

The Way Home

The three princesses climbed inside the
van and untied the horses one by one.
Then they led them carefully out and
round the corner of the lane. Lottie
guided Twinkle, talking soothingly to her
and stroking her velvety coat. Twinkle
stopped shivering and nibbled at Lottie's
hair.

"The trouble is they'll know something's
wrong as soon as they drive off," said
Amina worriedly. "The van won't feel as

heavy as it did before."

Lottie bit her lip. "We need to put something heavy inside." She looked around and noticed some large rocks lying in the moonlit stream.

"I'll get those stones! They'll make it feel heavier." She quickly climbed down the bank and pulled one large rock out of the stream. She passed it up to Amina, who loaded it into the van.

She grabbed another rock. Her feet were wet and her hands felt freezing, but she didn't care. The only thing that mattered was rescuing the horses.

Altogether the girls loaded five large rocks into the van. Then they shut the door and rushed back round the corner to the horses just as Lady Slyden returned.

"Hurry up, you fool!" Lady Slyden told the man. "We don't know who else is out here. Do you *want* to be caught?"

The two figures dived into the van and drove away at top speed.

A shadow slipped along the lane and Rosalind appeared in front of them, grinning.

"They couldn't work out what my noise was and then they got spooked," she said.

One of the horses let out a loud chuckling whinny, sending the girls into fits of laughter.

Lottie and Twinkle led the group of princesses and horses up the lane and through the fields. When she reached her own field, Twinkle galloped round and round, swishing her tail.

"You're happy to be home, aren't you, Twinkle?" laughed Lottie.

They were met at the stables by Peter, who was waving his torch about and looking frantic.

"What happened?" he said. "I came

down here to check on the horses and some of them were missing."

"Lady Slyden tried to steal them," said Lottie. "Even poor Twinkle."

Peter shone his torch on to the animals. "She chose all the racehorses," he said angrily. "She probably wanted to sell them to make lots of money."

"I remember Queen Sofia saying that Twinkle might be a racehorse, too, one day," said Isabella.

"I can see why." Lottie grinned as Twinkle galloped past with her mane flying.

Peter began settling the horses back into their stalls. Lottie managed to catch Twinkle and lead her back to the stables. Twinkle's mother whinnied and nuzzled her little foal and then they snuggled down together on the hay. Twinkle closed her eyes and lay down her head. The

white star on her forehead gleamed in the moonlight.

"I'm so glad you're safe again after such a worrying night," Lottie told the little foal.

She stroked her soft ears one more time and then shut the stall door.

"I'll just get the horses some extra feed," said Peter, hurrying out of the stables.

Lottie noticed that the other princesses were all helping with the horses too. Rosalind was smiling widely, Amina had stopped looking nervous and Isabella hadn't tripped over anything for ages. Something wonderful had happened to them all, ever since their rings had glowed.

Lottie looked down at her glistening ruby. *Jewels with special powers*, Emily had called them. She pressed the red stone and it blazed with light. "Calling all

Rescue Princesses!" she whispered into it.

The jewels on the other girls' rings lit up too. The sapphire, the emerald and the yellow topaz all glowed brightly.

"Wow!" cried Amina.

The princesses crowded together to look at each other's glowing rings.

"Your voice sounded really clear just then," said Rosalind. "And it came right out of my ring."

"Mine too," said Isabella.

"They're working perfectly," said Lottie, grinning. "We pulled off a great rescue tonight. It's almost as if these rings made us magical, too."

"I don't think our rescue was magic," said Isabella. "I think it was teamwork. Maybe the rings couldn't work properly until we started working together."

Lottie smiled at her. "Maybe you're right!"

The sky began to lighten as morning came closer.

Peter came back in with a wheelbarrow full of hay. He stopped and looked at the princesses. "I just noticed how funny you all look," he said. "What are you wearing?"

"These are our black dancing dresses," Rosalind told him. "Very handy for sneaking across the palace garden at night!"

Peter looked a little confused. "I guess wearing black does camouflage you in the dark."

"Exactly!" said Isabella. "And now we'd better go. The grown-ups will wake up soon."

"Thanks for bringing the horses back to me," said Peter. "You're not really ordinary princesses, are you?"

"Not really!" laughed Lottie.

The princesses grinned at him. Then they linked their arms together and hurried back across the field towards the palace.

The Final Performance

Ally brought the princesses a delicious breakfast of warm rolls and honey, with tall glasses of strawberry milkshake. The girls sat at a table in Lottie's room and tucked into the food. All the excitement and ninja moves of the night before had made them extremely hungry.

"Is it the last performance of the Dance Festival today?" said Isabella, helping herself to another roll.

"Yes it is! And we still need to sort out

our costumes," said Amina.

Rosalind brushed the crumbs off her hands and rummaged through the pile of dance dresses on Lottie's bed. She grinned at the others. "How about this?" She pulled a lime-green leotard out of the pile and held it up to show them.

"No way!" laughed Isabella. "That reminds me of Queen Sofia's hat."

Finally they agreed on golden dance dresses with black jazz shoes. After breakfast, they changed into the costumes and brushed their hair. Then they walked downstairs to the hall, where the final performance would take place.

Rows of chairs had been set out for the audience. The seats were already filling up with kings, queens and other royalty. Everyone had put on their most splendid robes and dresses, and crowns and tiaras sparkled everywhere.

The princesses paused in the doorway, suddenly nervous about all the pairs of eyes that would be watching their dance routine.

"Queen Sofia?" A king in a blue turban bowed low. "Would you like me to find Lady Slyden and tell her we're ready to begin? She seems to be missing again."

Queen Sofia turned round, her lime-green hat quivering. "There's no need," she said firmly. "I found out some shocking news from my stable boy this morning. Lady Slyden has been unkind to the horses I lent her and last night she tried to steal some of them. I've sent her a message telling her never to return to my palace, and she's lucky that I haven't had her arrested. How dare she behave so cruelly to my animals?"

The princesses beamed at each other.

"Peter must have told Queen Sofia all

about Lady Slyden," whispered Lottie. "Good for him!"

"Good morning, princesses!" boomed Queen Sofia, seeing them standing together. "I'd like you to begin the grand performance. What kind of dance have you chosen?"

"Disco," chorused the princesses.

"Disco?" repeated Queen Sofia. "Excellent! I am quite in the mood for a little boogie."

Hiding their giggles, the princesses took up their starting positions. The hall fell silent. Then the beat of the song began. The princesses stepped and twirled, remembering all their dance moves perfectly. At the end the audience clapped and cheered, and the girls dropped graceful curtsies.

Their act was followed by tap dances, ballet dances and the princes' hornpipe.

After the grand performance had finished, Lottie looked over to the door in the corner that led out into the garden. She beckoned to the others and, while the grown-ups were still chatting, they slipped out of the door and raced across the lawn.

Lottie reached the gate first and climbed over it into the field.

"I wonder if the horses are tired after their adventure last night," said Amina.

Just then, Twinkle came trotting out of the stables. She whinnied excitedly when she saw them and galloped round and round in circles.

"Stop, Twinkle! You're making me dizzy," laughed Rosalind.

Twinkle stopped galloping and nibbled Lottie's hair.

"I think Twinkle's trying to say thank you," said Amina.

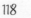

"You're welcome, Twinkle." Lottie rubbed the little foal's velvety nose. "Now I can't wait to do the next rescue!"

"And we could find out more about the lost *Book of Ninja* that Ally talked about," suggested Rosalind.

"And whatever we do, we'll do it together." Isabella held out her hand with its special ring.

"Together!" said the others, putting their hands on top of hers.

The jewels in their rings lit up for a moment, making the girls catch their breath.

Twinkle whinnied and lifted up her front leg too.

"You're joining in, Twinkle!" Lottie hugged her. "You really are the loveliest foal in the world!"

Can't wait for
The Rescue Princesses's next
daring animal adventure?

The Lost Gold

Turn the page for
a sneaky peek!

Chapter One

The Blue Butterfly

Princess Isabella crept through the rainforest with a small monkey riding on her shoulder. Parrots squawked to each other in the treetops and water drops from the last rain shower glinted on the broad leaves.

Isabella's curly brown hair was loosely tied up with a ribbon and her dark eyes were determined. The butterfly that she was following had landed on a leaf and was flexing its beautiful wings. She held her breath, slowly lifting up her camera.

It looked so perfect. The shiny wings were sky-blue with velvety black edges. She'd been trying to take a photo of a blue morpho butterfly for weeks and this was her chance!

"Stay really still, Petro," she whispered to the little monkey. "This will make a great picture!"

She peered through the viewfinder, holding her finger just above the button. The butterfly looked quite small. If only she could get a little closer. She took a tiny step towards it, but her foot caught on a tree root and she stumbled. She grabbed at a branch to save herself but it snapped. Petro leapt off her shoulder, chattering crossly, and Isabella landed on the ground on her hands and knees.

Disturbed by the noise, the blue butterfly flew away into the treetops, its wings shimmering in the dappled sunlight.